MW00904497

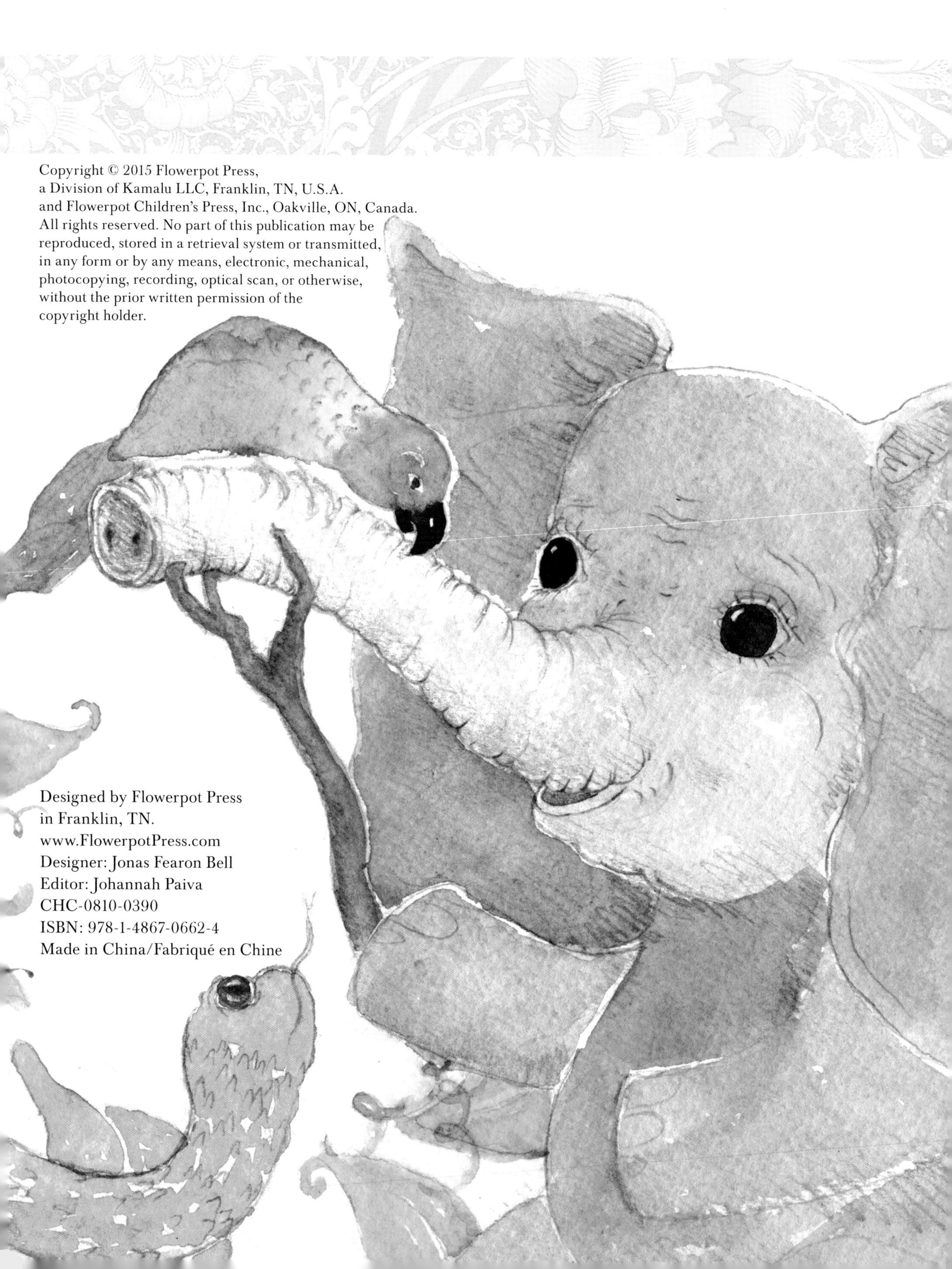

Designed by Flowerpot Press
in Franklin, TN.
www.FlowerpotPress.com
Designer: Jonas Fearon Bell
Editor: Johannah Paiva
CHC-0810-0390
ISBN: 978-1-4867-0662-4
Made in China/Fabriqué en Chine

Just So Stories

How the Elephant Got Her Trunk

Rudyard Kipling

Retold by
Stephanie P. Gilman

Illustrated by
T. G. Tjornehoj

"In memory of my sweet sister, Rhonda West, who knew I was a writer long before I did."
– SPG

Flowerpot Press
Toronto • Nashville

Have you ever WONDERED how the elephant got a long trunk?

It all started with a little elephant named Ellie who had, instead of a trunk, a stubby nose. This didn't seem funny at the time, since that's how elephants used to look.

Ellie was very inquisitive. That means she WONDERED about everything.

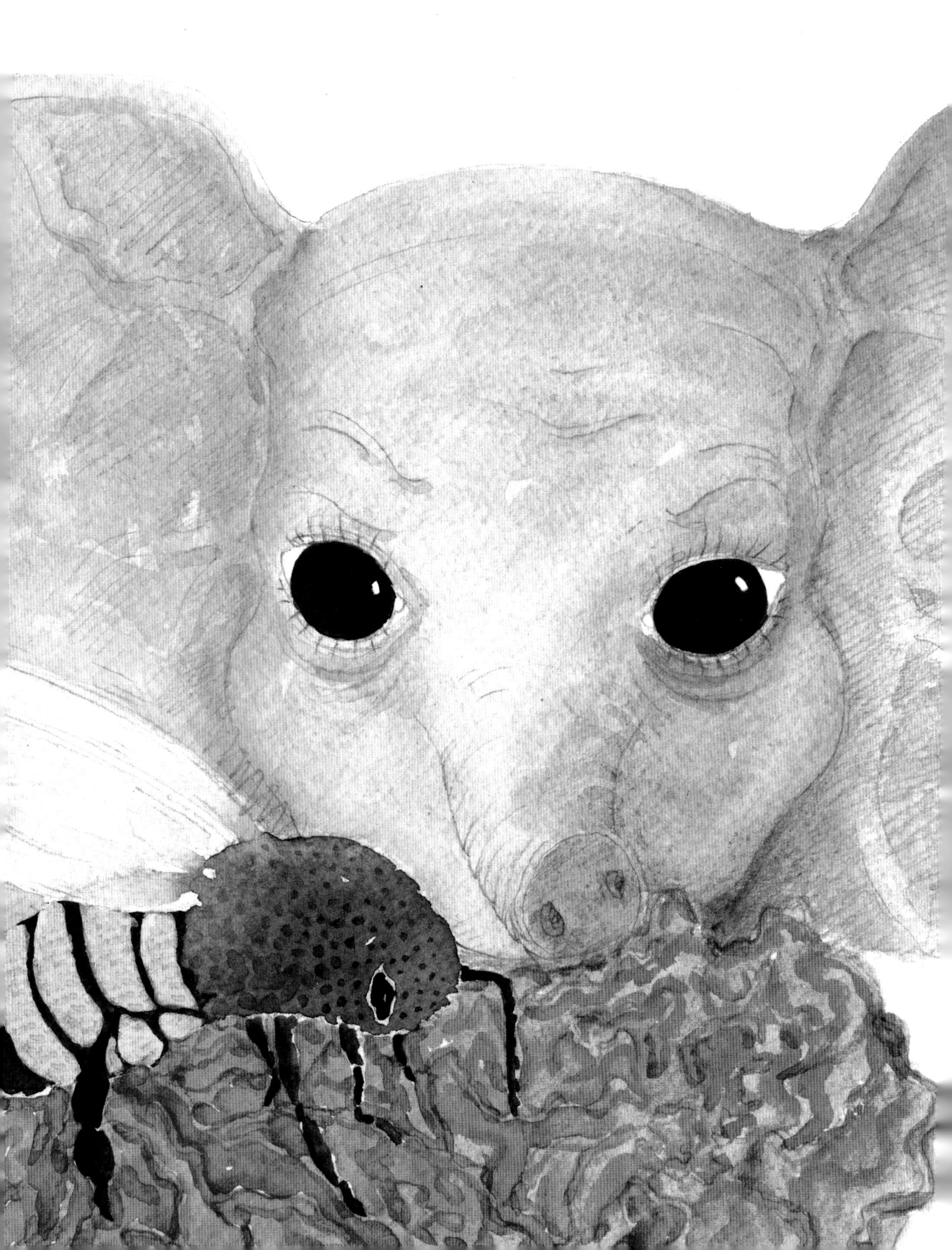

One day, Ellie sat WONDERING about all the WONDERFUL things she didn't understand. Just then, Aunt Ostrich trotted by. Ellie asked, "Aunt Ostrich, where did *you* get those long tail feathers, and why is *my* tail so very short?"

Aunt Ostrich raised her eyebrows. "That is not a question for a young elephant. Now, go do what elephants do." And off she ran, leaving a cloud of white feathers in her dust.

Ellie frowned. "What's neat about elephants?" she WONDERED. "I can't even grow tail feathers!"

At dinner, Ellie asked her mother, "Mama, what does a crocodile have for dinner?"

Mother Elephant stamped her big foot. "Ellie, why do you care what crocodiles eat? Please finish your dinner, dear."

Ellie's ears drooped. None of her WONDERINGS were getting any real answers.

The next day, Ellie rose early and headed out on a walk to see Sir Parrot the Wiser.

Once she got to the forest she called, "*Sir Paaaaaarrot!*" Then she tiptoed (as best as an elephant can tiptoe) through the trees, searching for the familiar old bird.

"My dear *Ellie-Ellie-Ellie*, what brings you to the rainforest *today-day-day*, *squuuuuaaaaawk?*" asked Sir Parrot as he swooped down from a tall tree and landed right on Ellie's head.

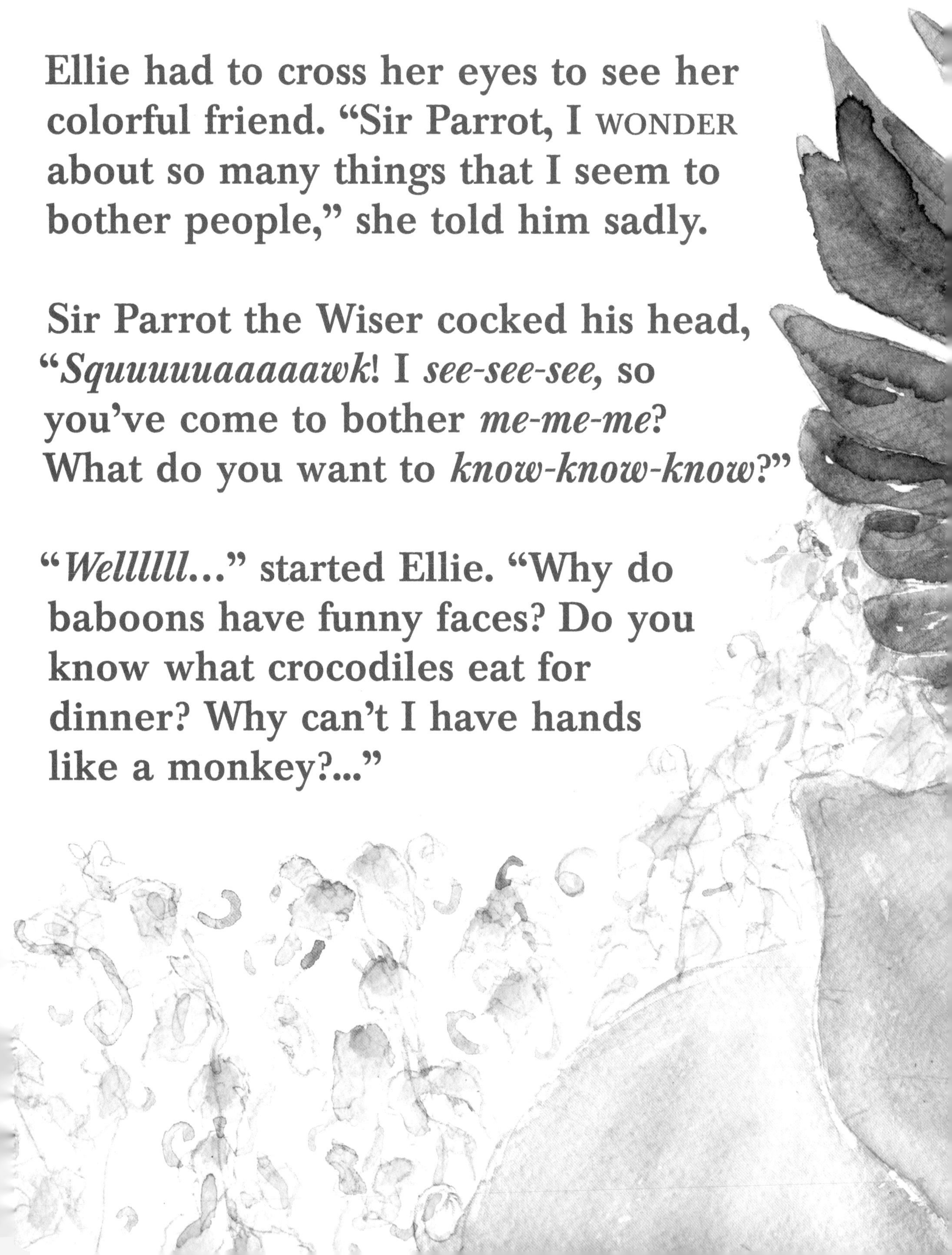

Ellie had to cross her eyes to see her colorful friend. "Sir Parrot, I WONDER about so many things that I seem to bother people," she told him sadly.

Sir Parrot the Wiser cocked his head, "*Squuuuuaaaaawk*! I *see-see-see,* so you've come to bother *me-me-me*? What do you want to *know-know-know*?"

"*Wellllll…*" started Ellie. "Why do baboons have funny faces? Do you know what crocodiles eat for dinner? Why can't I have hands like a monkey?..."

Sir Parrot squawked and exclaimed, "Sorry! One question a *day-day-day*!"

Ellie thought carefully about what she WONDERED most. "Ok, what does a crocodile eat for dinner?"

Sir Parrot the Wiser thought for a moment. "I suggest you ask a *crocodile-dile-dile* yourself at the Limpopo River. But don't get too close. Ask him from *afar-far-far. Squuuuuaaaaawk*!"

"Thanks, Sir Parrot! I'm going to ask him right now!"

And off she went.

As Ellie neared the river, she met a snake napping in the sunshine. She WONDERED if the snake knew where to find the crocodile.

"*Scuse me,*" Ellie whispered, WONDERING if the snake even *had* ears. The snake didn't answer, so she said quite a bit louder, "*Ex-cuuuuuse* me!!!"

The snake jumped high into the air and landed hard back on the rock. "Who *goesssssss* there?!" the annoyed snake hissed.

“Ever so sorry,” Ellie apologized. “But I’m trying to find a crocodile, and Sir Parrot the Wiser told me to come to this river.”

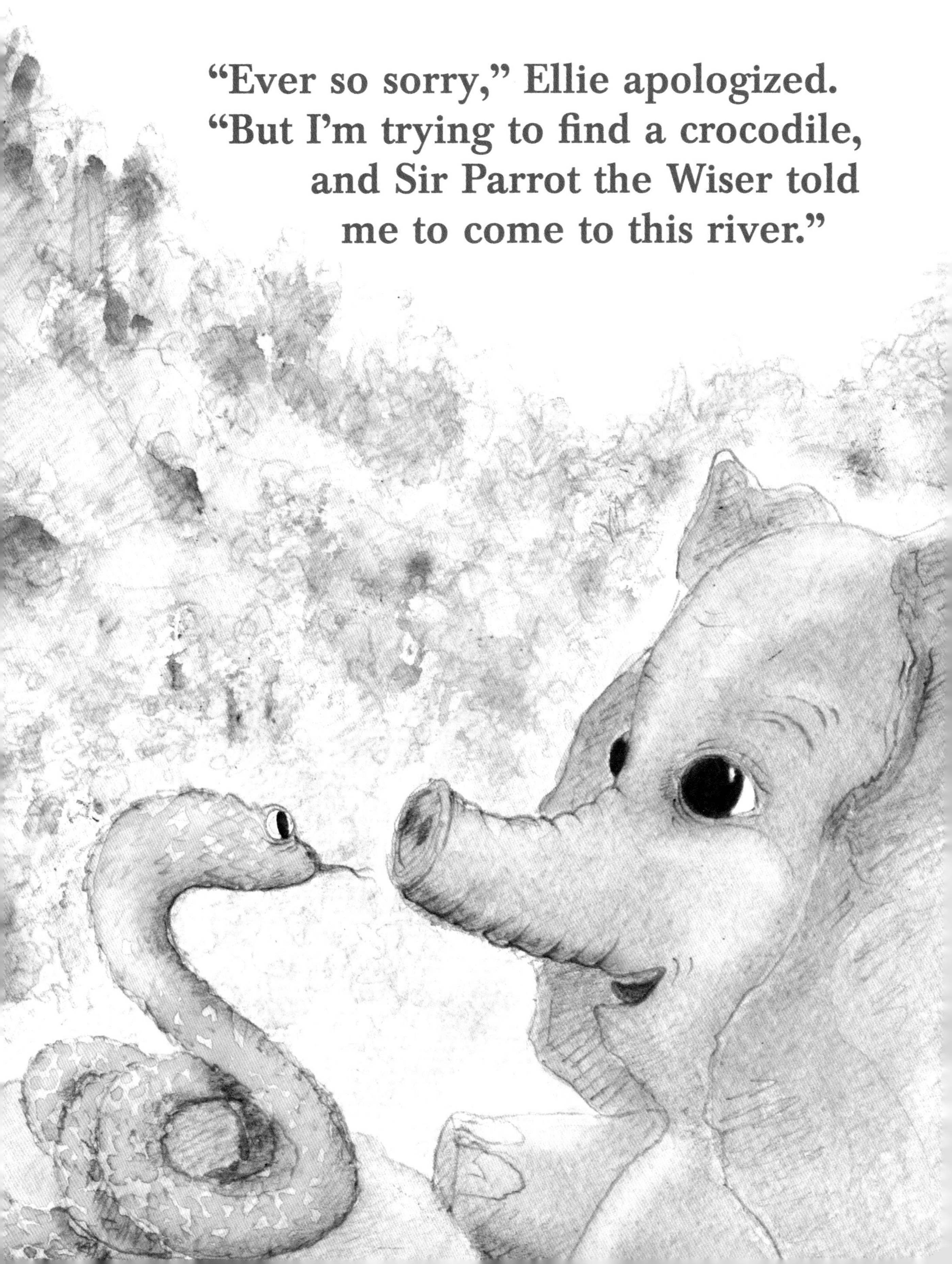

The snake curled back up into his tight coil. "Never you mind the crocodile," he said, closing his eyes. "*Sssssstay* away from him."

Ellie plopped down, feeling dejected. As she was WONDERING what to do next, a deep voice nearby called, "So, you're looking for the crocodile, you say?"

Ellie jumped up. "Oh yes! Do you know where I can find one? I'm WONDERING what they eat!" she asked excitedly.

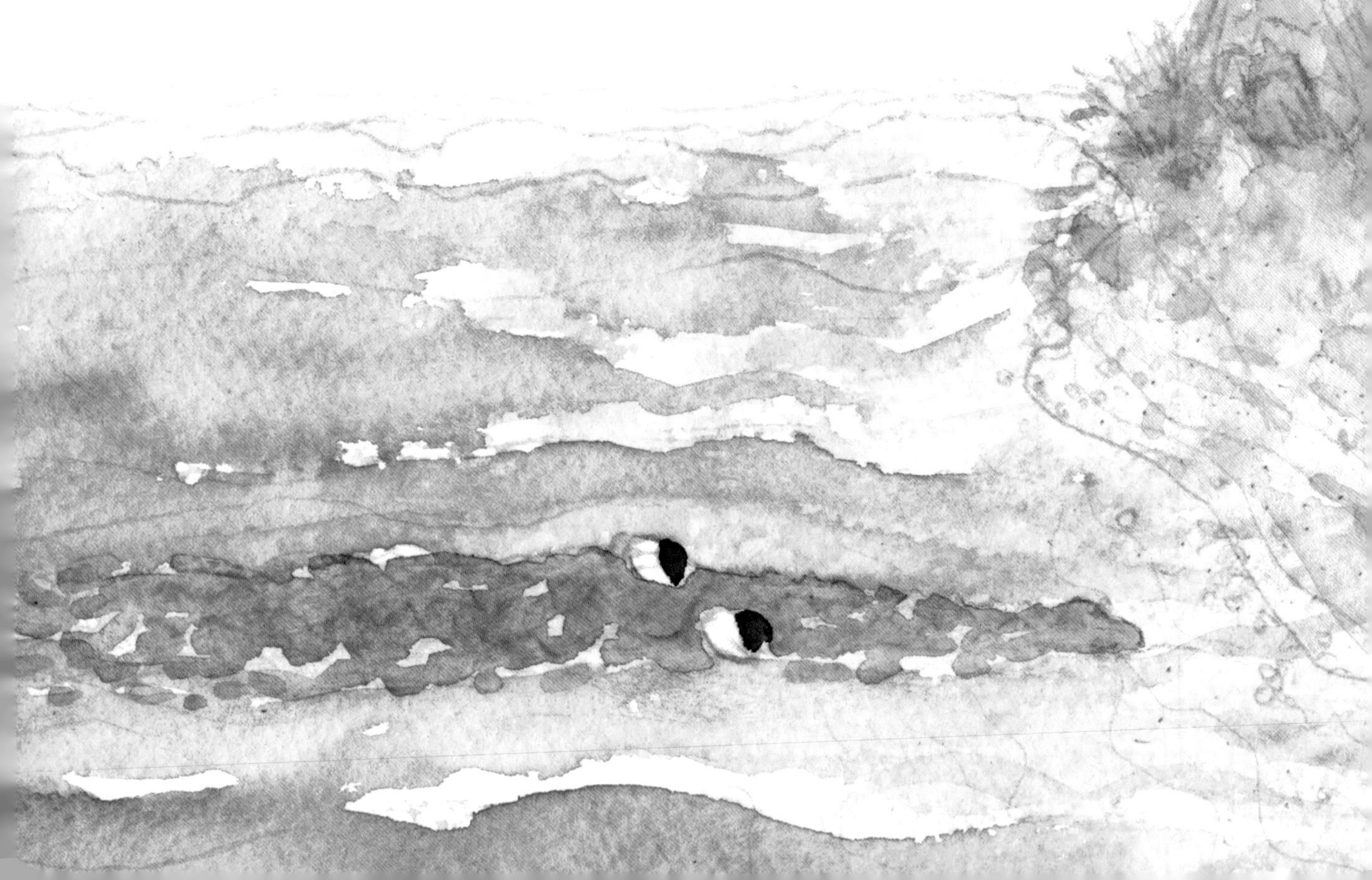

Two eyes poked out of the water, followed by a long snout with sharp teeth. "I can help you, for I am a crocodile."

Ellie was so excited. "It's you! I'm so happy to meet you!" Ellie said. "I've been WONDERING all day about what you eat!"

"What we eat is a very well kept secret. Come close, and I'll whisper it to you."

Forgetting Sir Parrot the Wiser's advice, Ellie leaned close to the crocodile's mouth, her feet sliding down the muddy bank.

"*Welllll*, today I think I'll have a young elephant!" And with a quick snap, the crocodile clamped his jaws over Ellie's unsuspecting stubby little nose.

"*Stob id!!!* This is *nod* a kind thing to do!!!" Ellie was beginning to WONDER why she ever sought his wisdom in the first place.

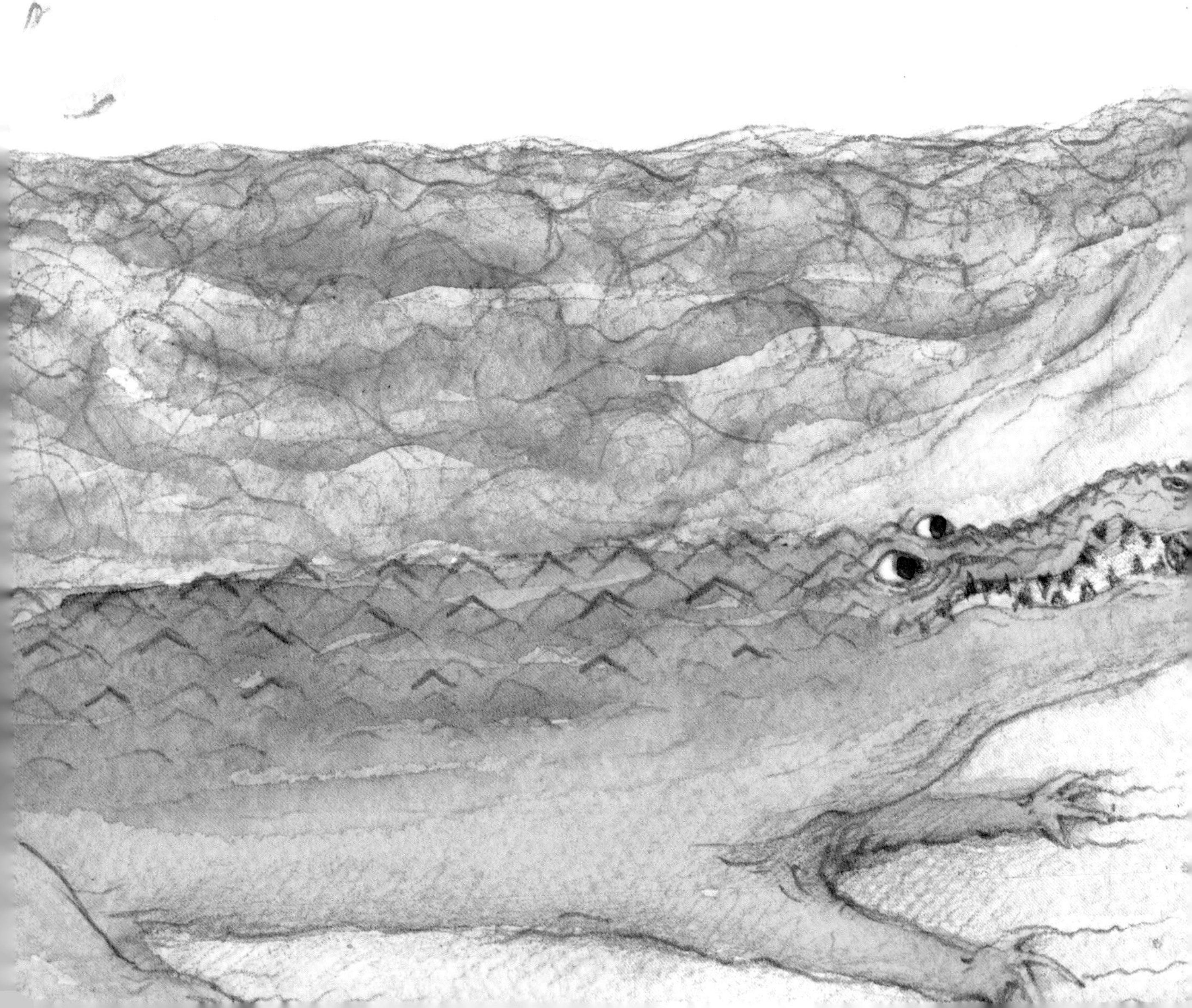

“Oh *goodnesssss,*” hissed the snake. “I can’t *sssssssssleep* with all this racket.” The snake then coiled around Ellie’s leg, and around a tree trunk, and he pulled as hard as he could.

The crocodile thrashed mightily, but the elephant and the snake working together were too strong for him. At last, he reluctantly let go and sank back into the water.

"*Pheeewww-y*!" Ellie huffed. That's when she realized her stubby nose had been stretched out very long indeed.

"*That'sssss* no longer a *nosssssse*, my dear elephant. It *sssssseems* you now have a trunk!" exclaimed the snake.

And so Ellie had a new and WONDERFUL trunk. It came in quite handy to pick up food and sticks. She could also suck in water and shoot it out like a hose. She could even see Sir Parrot without crossing her eyes.

While everyone chuckled at Ellie's new trunk, she was glad to have it…even if she did have to wrestle a crocodile to get it. "I WONDER," thought Ellie, "why all elephants don't want one."

And it turned out they did!

Like
Ellie, do you
WONDER about
many things?
That's great!
Just make sure you
ask an adult for the
answers and not a
crocodile. (I don't
think you'd like a
trunk as much as
Ellie does.)